**"What if it *is* Rocky?"
Dee Ellen said
in a whispery voice.
"I don't think
you're supposed to
disturb the dead."**

A sliver of breeze blew Monica's bangs back across her eyes. She looked up at the house and a thought chilled her. *Was living in that place going to do spooky things to her partner's mind?* Dee Ellen didn't have much control over her brain. Was she going to start acting strange?

"But this can't be a ghost!" Monica shrieked. "What do we know about chasing ghosts?"

Dee Ellen drifted slowly upward into a sitting position. Her eyes were huge blurry blobs in the center of her glasses. "We could ask an expert," she said. . . .

Books by Judith Hollands

Bowser the Beautiful
The Ketchup Sisters: The Rescue of the Red-Blooded Librarian
The Ketchup Sisters: The Deeds of the Desperate Campers
The Ketchup Sisters: The Secret of the Haunted Doghouse
The Like Potion
The Nerve of Abbey Mars

Available from MINSTREL BOOKS

THE KETCHUP S·I·S·T·E·R·S™

THE SECRET OF THE HAUNTED DOGHOUSE

JUDITH HOLLANDS

Illustrated by Dee deRosa

A MINSTREL® BOOK

PUBLISHED BY POCKET BOOKS

New York   London   Toronto   Sydney   Tokyo   Singapore

A MINSTREL PAPERBACK *ORIGINAL*

A Minstrel Book, published by
POCKET BOOKS, a division of Simon & Schuster Inc.
1230 Avenue of the Americas, New York, NY 10020

ISBN: 0-671-66812-9

First Minstrel Books printing May 1990

10 9 8 7 6 5 4 3 2 1

A MINSTREL BOOK and colophon are registered trademarks
of Simon & Schuster Inc.

Printed in the U.S.A.

For Matthew,
who loves all spooky things

THE SECRET
OF THE
HAUNTED
DOGHOUSE

CHAPTER ONE

Right before school started, the Zellers bought the old McMurty place. Nobody had lived in it for years. And lots of people said it was haunted.

Monica Tully was climbing the long row of steps up to the house. Dee Ellen Zeller waved down from the front porch. "So what do you think?" she called.

Monica stopped at the top of the steps. The house sat before her like something big and ugly and alive. She started on up to the porch.

"I guess your father likes lots of windows," Monica said.

Like long, skinny eyes, she thought.

"And a big wraparound porch," she said.

Like a huge, drooping smile, she thought.

"And green shingles," she said.

Like lizard scales, she thought.

"My father likes anything old," said Dee Ellen. "He's fixing up the inside. But he had to hire someone to clear out all the bushes and vines."

Monica shuddered as she looked around. "It's huge," she said. "Did you find a good place for the Ketchup Sisters' office?"

The Ketchup Sisters was Monica's and Dee Ellen's detective name. They were working their way up to being famous detectives.

"How about those lion statues by the bottom steps?" Dee Ellen suggested. "You could sit on one side and I could sit on the other."

Monica blew her floppy bangs out of her eyes and frowned. She wasn't sure. She wondered if customers would like sitting under the jaws of a lion.

2

Dee Ellen trotted down the steps. She had ketchup on one corner of her mouth. She was always eating some ketchup-covered snack. And her mother made her drink eight glasses of water a day. Monica spent lots of time eating, drinking, and going to the bathroom with Dee Ellen.

"Come on," Dee Ellen said. "I can't wait to show you what's out back." As she shuffled off, her sandals slapped against her pink socks.

Monica followed Dee Ellen along the side of the house. "We probably won't be needing an office anyway," Monica said. "I bet we find our next case any day now."

"Do you really think so?" Dee Ellen said limply. She kept on walking. "Maybe we should take a break."

Monica nearly choked. "What? But, Dee Ellen, we're just getting good! Our next case could be the one that'll make us famous forever!"

Dee Ellen turned and planted a hand on her hip. Her long T-shirt was hanging in big, droopy wrinkles. "I don't want to be famous," she said. "I'd just get stomach cramps."

Monica stared at the letters on Dee Ellen's T-shirt. It said BENNY'S BAIT SHOP and had a picture of a leaping fish. Sometimes her partner was so unpeppy, it made her worry. And she wished she'd be more careful about her clothes. Famous detectives probably didn't go around in pink socks and fish shirts.

"But, Dee Ellen—" Monica began. Then she stopped and peeked around her partner's shoulder. "Gosh," she gasped. "What are all those?"

They'd reached the garden at the back of the house. White-eyed statues stood everywhere on the huge sloping lawn.

Dee Ellen bounced out onto the grass and threw her arms open wide. "Aren't they

4

something?" she said. "Mr. McMurty did them all."

Monica glanced quickly away from all the still, silent faces. "Great," she said as a shiver snaked down her spine. "But doesn't it bother you? The way people talk about this house?"

"My dad says that's just stories," Dee Ellen called. She was on the far side of the garden, wading in some tall grass. "And that I shouldn't let them bother me. Look what I found here yesterday."

Monica hurried over to Dee Ellen. A statue of a small dog sat on a square stone base. "Rocky," Monica read, peering at the carved letters.

"And see what's over here," Dee Ellen said.

Monica followed her up to the side yard. There, tucked into the branches of an over-overgrown hedge, was a little, lopsided house.

Faded letters were painted over the door.

5

"Rocky," Monica said again. "Dee Ellen, I bet Rocky was Mr. McMurty's dog. And this was his doghouse."

The branches beside the doghouse suddenly began to shake and wave. Monica grabbed a fistful of Dee Ellen's shirt. "Dee Ellen!" she croaked. "Somebody's hiding in those bushes!"

CHAPTER TWO

Nola Abbott tumbled out at their feet.

Monica groaned. Nola was such a nosy brat. Whenever the Ketchup Sisters worked on a case, Nola got in the way. Maybe she was jealous. But mostly she was just a brat.

"I forgot to tell you," Dee Ellen said. "She lives right across the street from me now."

Nola scrambled up and looked at them with squinty eyes. This wasn't hard for Nola. Her ponytails were pulled very tight. "Did anything creepy happen yet?" she asked. "Did I miss any ghosts or anything?"

8

Dee Ellen began to shake her head. "We just got here ourselves," she said.

Nola pointed suddenly at the doghouse. "E-e-u," she squealed. "Is that haunted, too?"

Monica couldn't help herself. "Oh, sure. Rocky's the guard dog around here. He does a good job, too. For a dog that's been dead fifty years."

Nola took a quick step back from the doghouse. "You mean he's a ghost? Gosh, a ghost dog. That sounds like a story out of *The National Star.*"

Nola dug into her pocket and pulled out a rumpled piece of newspaper. She unfolded it and waved it under Monica's nose. At the top it said, THE HOUSE THAT WANTED OUR BRAINS.

"This place took over *the minds* of the people who lived there," Nola said. "They ended up like screaming blobs of Jell-O."

Monica snatched the paper and neatly folded it up. "That couldn't happen to us," she said clearly. "We're the Ketchup Sisters. We found out who was after you at Camp

9

Mini-ta-ha. And we helped catch a jewel robber."

"Big deal," Nola said. "My mom told me that jewel robber was hardly even a crook. He didn't go to jail. They just made him build birdhouses down at the park."

Monica's blood boiled as she balled one hand into a fist. "You—You'd better watch out," she sputtered. "Or I'll send Rocky out looking for you!"

"Hey!" called a sharp voice. "What's going on?"

Nearby, a tall boy was putting a lock on the toolshed door. He tossed a rake onto one shoulder and walked quickly toward them. "You kids shouldn't be hanging around here," he said in a crabby voice.

Nola made a face at the boy and bulged her nostrils. "Shut up, Brian," she said.

"Who is that?" Monica asked. She leaned close to Dee Ellen's ear. "Your baby-sitter?"

"No," Dee Ellen said. "My dad hired him to work on the garden."

The sound of shouting made them all look down toward the street. From the side yard, they could see a noisy truck rattling up to the curb. It was pulling a long platform behind it. Monica's sister was sitting on the back edge with a group of chattering teenagers.

"It's Page!" Monica said. She waved her arms over her head.

"Page?" said the crabby boy. "Page Tully? Is she coming up here?"

The boy didn't wait for an answer. Instead he scurried away, disappearing around the side of the house.

That's funny, Monica thought. The boy almost acted scared. Then Monica noticed the big green house towering over them. *It's the house,* she thought. That house could make anybody act creepy. It already had her making up ghost stories.

"Come on, Monica!" Page called. She jumped from the back of the truck. "We're supposed to go home now."

A banner was tacked along one side of the truck. It said GO WILDCATS in red painted letters. "Wildcats" was the nickname of the football team.

Nola started bouncing up and down like a yo-yo. "That's for the pep rally float," she cried. "I get to ride with the cheerleaders and the football players."

Monica rolled her eyeballs. "We know," she said. Every year there was a big pep rally and parade. This year Nola's mother was dressing her up as Little Miss Football. Nola had been showing off her costume for weeks.

"Gotta go," Monica said to Dee Ellen. She began to wind her way down the sloping hill to the street. "I'm coming, Page," she called to her sister.

Page and her friend Jolene stood on the sidewalk, waiting for her. As the noisy truck pulled away, all the teenagers hollered and waved.

Monica waved, too. She felt important, standing there with two popular high school kids. "So what's happening?" she asked brightly.

Page and Jolene suddenly looked as if

Monica were a disease germ. They hurried on ahead, whispering behind their hands.

Monica dug her hands into her pockets. That's the way Page was lately. She was too busy being a teenager to notice her own sister. But Monica had Page's secrets all figured out. She'd been studying the clues.

Hadn't Page been changing her hairdo every day?

Hadn't she been whispering about someone named K.T.?

Hadn't Monica seen her hugging a picture of the varsity soccer team?

It was all perfectly clear. To a kid with detective blood beating through her body. Page Tully was in love.

CHAPTER THREE

When school started, everyone was talking about Dee Ellen's house. A crowd of kids waited by the lockers each morning. By the third day it took up half the hall.

"Tell us about the screaming statue," asked Freddy Beesmore when Monica walked up. He had one arm clamped around his little brother's shoulders.

"Who told you that?" Monica asked. "Nola?"

"I heard there's blood dripping down the walls," said a kid in the back.

"And vampire bones in the cellar," said somebody else.

All the kids stood, watching Monica with eyes as round as pie plates.

Just then Dee Ellen shuffled up, carrying her tote bag over her shoulder. It said NATALIE'S NUT HOUSE on one side. Under the letters, a lady peanut was doing the can-can.

Dee Ellen eyed Monica and looked perfectly miserable.

Stomach cramps, Monica thought. Dee Ellen probably hated crowds.

"Give her room," Monica ordered, waving some kids aside. Monica liked crowds. They made her feel important. Being important and famous was much better than being a plain old kid. She couldn't understand why Dee Ellen didn't think so.

Suddenly a big boy pushed through all the kids. He had bright yellow hair and was wearing cracked sunglasses. He handed a note to Monica.

"Just in case," the boy said in a low voice. Then he walked off, snapping the fingers of one hand.

"Isn't that kid in the gifted program?" said Freddy.

Their new teacher, Miss Berty, leaned into the hallway. "Come on, children," Miss Berty said. She clapped her hands as if they were chickens in a road. "Into the room, now."

The little crowd headed toward the doorway. Monica could still hear them mumbling about fangs and boiled brains.

Monica turned and slammed her locker door. Behind it a person was pressed flat against the wall. It was Nola. She shoved a china pig at Monica's stomach.

"Give this to him," Nola squeaked.

Monica let the pig fall into her hands.

"He came to my window last night," Nola went on. "He said, 'Give me your piggy bank.' He must have known I got forty dollars for my birthday."

Monica looked into the pig's bulgy eyes. It had long curly eyelashes and smiling red lips.

Nola pushed away from the wall and slapped herself up against Monica's body.

Nola was a pretty short kid. Monica could feel her breath on her chin.

"I would have given it to him," Nola said. "But I got scared and screamed. He can have it! Just promise you'll make him stay away!"

"But who was it?" Monica asked. "Who did you see?"

Nola bunched up wads of Monica's shirt with both hands. "Don't pretend," she wheezed. "You know. I saw him run back into Dee Ellen's garden."

A teeny little voice came from behind Monica's back. "I was going to tell you," Dee Ellen said. "I saw him last night, too."

"But who?" Monica demanded. She looked from Nola to Dee Ellen. "Who? *Who?*"

"It was Rocky," Dee Ellen said.

Nola nodded and her ponytails bobbed up and down. "That's right," she said. "He was big and yellow and hairy. I know a spooky monster when I see one."

"Rocky?" Monica warbled. "But Rocky's a

19

cocker spaniel! And he's been dead for fifty years!"

Miss Berty stepped into the hallway again. "Girls!" she boomed. "Into the classroom this minute!"

Nola snatched up her books and headed for Miss Berty. Dee Ellen scurried behind her. The back of her shirt said MY DOG LOVES PEPPY PUPPY SUPPER. Monica came last, carrying the china pig.

Monica's head was pounding as she stuffed the pig into her desk. The Ketchup Sisters had found their next case. Who was after Nola's piggy bank? A crook in a fur coat? Or a very spooky cocker spaniel?

The note from the boy in the sunglasses was still crumpled in Monica's hand. She unfolded it. It said:

P. Moon, Expert
strange Creatures and Ghosts

CHAPTER FOUR

As soon as school was over, Monica and Dee Ellen rushed to the Zellers' house. Dee Ellen stopped Monica as they were crossing the patio.

"How about a snack?" Dee Ellen said. "I think we've got Potato Doodles and Crunchy Buddy Bars. When Mom's away, Dad buys us junk food."

Monica made a face. "How can you think about food now?" she asked.

"I think about food all the time," Dee Ellen said. "I hardly even try. Maybe my brain does it for me."

"Well, try to control your brain," Monica said. "If you're going to be a detective, you've got to think like one."

Dee Ellen threw her skinny arms into the air. "But I can't think at all when I'm hungry!" she whined.

Monica ended up waiting on the patio while Dee Ellen raided her kitchen. When she came out, Monica led the way to the doghouse.

"This could be the big case we've been waiting for," Monica said. "Some crook's running around making people think he's a ghost. We could get in *The National Star* when we solve this. Can't you picture it? 'Schoolgirls Solve Secret of Spooky Spaniel.'"

"But how would we do that?" Dee Ellen asked.

"By digging up the facts," Monica said. "By figuring out what's really going on. Detectives call it uncovering the naked truth."

Monica dropped to her knees and crawled

up to the doghouse. "It looks empty," she said. She inched forward, stretching to peer inside.

Dee Ellen was standing on a big flat rock. "He could be in there," she said in a funny, spooky voice. "Waiting for darkness. Maybe you can't see him in the daytime."

The hole of the doghouse suddenly looked like a wide, howling mouth. Monica shrank back. "For Pete's sake, Dee Ellen," she said. "Do you really think your doghouse is haunted?"

Dee Ellen's face was as white as uncooked pizza crust. "Well, why not?" she asked. *The National Star* had a story about a haunted haystack."

Monica scrambled up and let out a big sigh. "But we're trying to find out what's really going on. Let everybody else holler about ghosts. We have to be logical."

Monica wasn't sure what logical meant. But that's what all the big-time detectives said on TV.

Monica began to pace in circles around the big rock. "Now go over it again," she ordered Dee Ellen. "Tell me what you saw."

"Well," Dee Ellen began. "At first I thought I saw a boy. But then when I looked again, it was Rocky. He was all yellow and hairy and huge."

Monica blew her bangs out of her eyes. "But don't you see?" she said. "That could be a nice regular crook. It could be somebody in a fur coat."

Dee Ellen sat there for a moment, staring at nothing. Then she sank back onto the rock and clasped her hands over her chest. She looked as still and white as one of the statues in the garden.

"But what if it *is* Rocky?" Dee Ellen said in a whispery voice. "I don't think you're supposed to disturb the dead."

A sliver of breeze blew Monica's bangs back across her eyes. She looked up at the house and a thought chilled her. *Was living in that place going to do spooky things to her partner's mind?* Dee Ellen didn't have much

24

control over her brain. Was she going to start acting strange?

"But this crook can't be a ghost!" Monica shrieked. "What do we know about chasing ghosts?"

Dee Ellen drifted slowly upward into a sitting position. Her eyes were huge blurry blobs in the center of her glasses. "We could ask an expert," she said.

CHAPTER FIVE

Dee Ellen went inside and made a phone call to P. Moon. Then they walked the three blocks to his house. "I don't like this," Monica grumbled. "Detectives are supposed to be logical. I know we can be logical if we try."

"Shhh," said Dee Ellen. "Just see what he says."

P. Moon was leaning against a battered fence, wearing the cracked sunglasses. "I've been waiting for you," he said in his funny, low-sounding voice.

He led them down a weedy sidewalk and into the center of his backyard. A huge wooden box-thing was standing on four un-even legs. "This is my office," P. Moon said. "I made it myself."

P. Moon swung himself up and crawled under a black curtain. The whole box-thing teetered on the uneven legs. Dee Ellen and Monica climbed in after him.

It was pretty dark inside. P. Moon flicked on two flashlights. He set them into water glasses and stood the glasses on the floor. The beams of light crossed each other in the center of the shadowy room.

Dee Ellen cleared her throat. "Did you find out anything about what I said? Anything about ghost dogs?"

P. Moon dropped onto the flattest-looking beanbag chair Monica had ever seen. He pulled up a metal wastebasket. "Ghost dogs . . ." he said, taking a book from the basket. "This should do it."

Monica leaned forward, straining to see the cover. Something swatted her in the face. A mobile with fuzzy spiders and plastic eyeballs swung from the center of the box.

Monica dropped into a frog squat. "Just tell us what you found," she said. "And make it fast."

"Some questions first," P. Moon said. He slid the sunglasses up onto his forehead. For some reason, they didn't fall back down. "Now, did the dog howl?" he asked.

Monica and Dee Ellen looked at each other. "No," Dee Ellen said.

"Did it have blood dripping from its fangs —right here?" P. Moon curled his top lip and pointed at his corner teeth.

"Are we still talking about a cocker spaniel?" Monica asked.

P. Moon let a finger slide down the page of the open book. "Maybe not," he said. "I think you might have a *weredog* on your hands."

"A *weredog?*" Monica cried. "There's no such thing!" She leaped forward and grabbed the book from the boy's hands.

Across the cover was printed the word WEREWOLVES. "I knew it!" Monica cried. "This isn't even about dogs. You're like

everyone else. You're just making up stories!"

P. Moon slid back farther into the beanbag chair. "Okay," he said. "So I didn't find anything yet. Maybe I need more time."

"Time?" Monica shrieked. "There's a crook after innocent kids' birthday money! We can't waste time. We've got to stop him!"

P. Moon nodded his head slightly and the sunglasses fell back over his eyes. "And I hear he's yellow and hairy all over," he said. He folded his arms over his chest.

"W-Well, yes," Monica stammered. "But a crook's a crook. If you think logically, this one could just need a shave."

"Maybe so," P. Moon said. He put his hands behind his neck and cracked his knuckles. "And maybe not. Some things aren't logical at all." His thin lips stretched into a very creepy smile. "And tonight there's a full moon."

Dee Ellen leaned around Monica's side. "A full moon?" she squeaked. "Isn't that when all kinds of weird things happen? Can't you give us any expert advice at all?"

P. Moon scratched his nose and lifted a finger. "Garlic," he said. "Garlic is the best ban against evil forces."

Monica had heard enough. *"Garlic!"* she said. She turned, crawled through the curtain, and jumped out onto the grass. "What are we supposed to do?" she called back. "Beat him with a pizza?"

A little girl was running across the lawn. "Another customer!" Monica cried. "Are you looking for P. Moon, the ghost expert?"

The little girl stuffed a finger into her mouth. "I just want Petey," she said. "He's my broth-uh."

Dee Ellen jumped from the box with Petey behind her. "So maybe I don't know everything," Petey Moon said. He leaned against his teetering office. "But if I had a ghost after my piggy bank, I know what I'd do."

Monica was dragging Dee Ellen down the weedy sidewalk. "What?" Dee Ellen asked, twisting to look back.

"I'd give it to him," said Petey Moon.

When they got to the front of the house, Monica threw her hands into the air. "Can we get down to work now?" Monica demanded. "Are you all done with this ghost stuff?"

Dee Ellen let her head fall against Monica's chest. "But tonight's a full moon," she blubbered. "I don't want to be alone if something weird is going to happen!" Dee Ellen snuffled loudly and wiped her nose on Monica's shirt. "Say you'll spend the night," she begged.

Monica nodded and patted her partner on the back. The McMurty house was getting to Dee Ellen, all right. She was turning into a blubbering blob of Jell-O.

Maybe Monica Tully would have to figure things out on her own.

CHAPTER SIX

Monica went home and packed her backpack. Then she stood staring at herself in her closet mirror.

Something very strange is going on at Dee Ellen's, Monica told herself. She could probably quit now. She could start screaming about ghosts like everyone else.

The Monica in the mirror stared back at her. *But you've got a mystery to solve,* she seemed to say.

Monica back-flopped onto her bed and looked at the ceiling. The Ketchup Sisters had a really big case on their hands this time.

A good detective wouldn't poop out now. A good detective would get busy and uncover the naked truth.

The door suddenly swung open wide. "Monica Tully!" Page cried, stomping in. "Have you been using my Dip 'n Set on your Popsicle-stick town?"

Monica sat straight up. "But Page," she whined. "That stuff dries like cement. Just think what it's doing to your hair!"

Jolene Katz came winding through the doorway, looking dreamy-eyed. "Can you stand it?" she said in a whispery voice. "Your sister has a date with Kirby Tuffs. Kirby Tuffs!" Jolene wailed, sinking back onto the bedspread. "He's the *president* of the junior class!"

Kirby Tuffs! Monica thought wildly. *K.T.!* She'd forgotten that her sister was in love. "A date?" she said. "When?"

"Right now," said Page. She squinted at her wristwatch. "I'm supposed to meet Kirby at Burger Bob's in fifteen minutes."

Page grabbed Monica's shoulders and pulled her from the bed. Page had another new hairdo. Her bangs were flipping sideways like an ocean wave.

"Say you'll help Mom with the dishes," Page begged. "I know it's my night. But please, Monica. I'll pay you!"

"But I wanted to go to Dee Ellen's right after dinner," Monica said.

Jolene flipped onto her belly and crawled to the end of the bed. "You're going to *Zeller's* place?" she asked. "Haven't you heard about the headless demon that moans at midnight?"

Monica stabbed a finger down into Jolene's face. "Another story!" she howled. "Doesn't anyone care about the naked truth?"

Page yanked on one end of the scarf in Jolene's hair. "Will you two stop all this silly stuff?" she said. "Something important is going on here. I have to decide what to wear!"

Page flounced out and Jolene got up to follow. Then she turned and gave Monica a long up-and-down look. "Weird kid," she muttered.

Monica stood watching as the door closed behind them. Then she went and took Nola's pig from her dresser top. She had to do something to uncover the facts. She tucked the pig into her backpack.

Petey Moon had given her an idea. Whoever was out in Dee Ellen's garden wanted Nola's piggy bank.

The Monica in the mirror stared at her from across the room. "So here's the plan," she said to her wide-eyed self. "We put the pig in the doghouse. Then we see who comes after it."

"Monica!" Mrs. Tully called from downstairs. "Come on, honey. Dinner's ready!"

Monica dragged her backpack from the bed. If the plan worked, they'd catch their crook tonight. Whoever it was. She wished that made her feel more logical. Instead of sweaty all over.

Dinner seemed to take forever. Monica was filling the dishwasher when somebody knocked at the back door. It was Petey Moon, wearing the cracked sunglasses. He had a baseball cap on backward over his yellow hair.

"I made this for you," Petey said. He pushed a lumpy something into Monica's hands.

Monica looked down. It was a bunch of garlics tied up with dirty shoelaces.

"I didn't have any string," Petey said.

"Detectives use brain power to solve cases," Monica said crisply. "Not garlics."

"Just in case," Petey said, smiling his creepy smile. Then he turned and strolled away, snapping the fingers of one hand.

Monica's backpack was sitting on the kitchen counter. For a minute she stood staring at the chain of lumpy little garlics. Then she unzipped the backpack and dropped the necklace inside. "Just in case," she said, peering in after it.

Fwap! The door beside Monica opened and slammed, making her jump. Page charged into the kitchen. Her nostrils were puffing in and out like a wild bull's.

"Why are you back?" Monica asked.

"It wasn't even a date!" Page cried, sounding totally insulted. "Kirby invited half the freshman class! The school mascot is missing. He wanted us to help find it before the parade tonight."

"The parade?" Monica said. "Is that tonight?"

Page slumped into a chair. "Yes," she grumbled. "And I wouldn't go near it for a million dollars."

The phone rang. "Page!" Mrs. Tully called from the other room. "It's for you."

Page picked up the kitchen phone and mumbled a few words. Then she hung up. "Mr. Zeller needs to go out for a little while," she said. "He wants me to baby-sit."

CHAPTER SEVEN

Monica was glad her sister was coming to the Zellers', too. Page was a pretty logical kind of person. She didn't go around talking about ghosts with empty eye sockets.

But Page did want to talk about something. All the way to the Zellers' she babbled on and on about Kirby Tuffs. "So I just left," Page said. "I walked right out of Burger Bob's. You can't blame me, can you?"

Monica blinked. "Uh—no," she stammered. She wondered if she should tell Page everything. Maybe Page would want to help catch the crook.

Pointy fingernails suddenly dug into Monica's arm and her sister stopped walking. "Oh gosh, Monica," Page sputtered. "Look —it's him."

Two boys were headed down the sidewalk toward them. "It's Kirby," Page whispered. She shoved a hand through her flipped-out bangs.

"Hey, Page," one of the boys called. "Where did you go? I was looking for you. We've only got two hours to find the missing mascot."

Monica looked at Kirby as he walked up. He had dark hair that curled over his collar and nice, foggy-gray eyes.

Page seemed puzzled. "But you had all those other kids," she said. "And now I have to baby-sit."

"Oh," said Kirby. "That's too bad." He looked down at his sneakers. Then up into Page's eyes. He looked. She looked back.

Monica waited. *He likes her,* she thought.

The other boy was holding a stack of

papers. He handed one to Kirby and pointed at Monica. "Ask the kid if she's seen anything," the boy said.

Kirby passed Monica the paper. It was a photocopy of the football team picture. Somebody had put a big black circle on it in crayon.

"But what's this?" Monica asked.

"It's the Bramley Wildcat," said Page. "Every year the seniors hide the wildcat costume from the juniors. The class that finds it gets to ride on the pep rally float."

Monica squinted at the crayon circle. A funny-looking animal stood inside it. He had one arm curled around a football player. In the other he held a long, yellow tail.

"The Bramley Wildcat," Monica whispered as her eyes bulged. "This is just somebody dressed up, right?"

Kirby laughed. "Well, sure. You didn't think it was real, did you?"

Monica didn't answer him. She was starting to feel excited all over.

"What is it, Monica?" Page asked. "Have you seen it?"

Monica looked up. "Well, no," she began. "I didn't, but—"

Beep! Beep! A horn blared as a car full of high school kids pulled up to the curb. The other boy ran down to it. "Come on, Kirby," he yelled. "Everybody's meeting back at Burger Bob's."

Kirby began to back away, smiling a nervous little smile. "Well, I've got to get going," he said to Page. He backed away a few more steps, then scurried down to the car.

Page watched him go. "Oh, I hope he's not mad," she whined. "What if he thinks I wanted to leave? Oh, I'll die. I'll just die."

Page began to walk quickly toward the Zellers'. Monica pounded along beside her. At last her sister stopped mumbling for a moment. "I've got to show this paper to Dee Ellen," Monica said.

Page stopped walking and gave her a blank look. "Huh? Oh, Dee Ellen. Sure. But you'd better talk to your other friend first."

"What friend?" Monica asked.

Page nodded toward someplace behind Monica's back. "The one in the little queen outfit," Page said. "She's over there, waving at you."

Monica turned and saw Nola on the sidewalk across the street. She was wearing her Little Miss Football outfit. On her head was a small golden crown. Monica stuffed the paper into her backpack and hurried across the street.

"Did you give Rocky the piggy bank?" Nola asked as Monica walked up.

"Not yet," Monica said. "I was going to take care of all that later."

Nola stepped so close, Monica could see hairs in her nose. "Be sure to give it to the right ghost," Nola warned. "That place is loaded with them. I heard my brother say there's a wildcat in the toolshed."

The words thundered across Monica's brain. "Did you say a 'wildcat in the toolshed'?" Monica repeated.

Nola's squinty eyes glittered and she

grinned from ear to ear. "Scary, huh?" she said. It's probably waiting to drag kids *to their doom.*"

Monica didn't waste another second. She turned and began walking. She walked faster. She ran. She raced across the street and up the steps to the Zellers'. On the top step she stopped. Her eyes slid slowly up to the house.

The long windows stared like empty eyes. The sagging porch smiled. Beneath the porch crisscrosses of wood looked like broken teeth.

Monica looked down and marched on toward the door. No house was going to make her into a quivering lump. Not when there was detective work to do.

And if what she was thinking was right, there was no reason to be scared. No reason at all.

CHAPTER EIGHT

Dee Ellen was sitting across from Monica in the Zellers' kitchen. "Why are you smiling like that?" Dee Ellen said. She was downing a glass of water and dipping pretzels into a puddle of ketchup.

"I've got something to show you," Monica whispered. She unzipped her backpack and began to rummage through it. The string of garlics fell onto the table.

"Monica," Dee Ellen cried. "You brought garlic! Does this mean you think Rocky is real?"

"No," Monica snapped. "Petey brought

that over. And never mind. You don't think that stuff works, do you?"

Dee Ellen gently lifted the necklace over her head. She smiled peacefully and fingered the garlics as if they were pearls.

Monica suddenly felt very jumpy. Dee Ellen was acting stranger every minute. She had to do something. Before her partner's mind was a goner.

"Look at this!" Monica shrieked. She jammed the paper at Dee Ellen. "Is this who you saw in the garden?"

Dee Ellen bent forward and stopped patting the garlics. "It's Rocky!" she said.

"Look again, Dee Ellen," Monica ordered. "Is that a cocker spaniel?"

Dee Ellen's forehead wrinkled up into wiggly lines. "What is that?" she said.

"It's the Bramley Wildcat!" Monica cried. She jumped to her feet. "Oh, Dee Ellen. That's what you saw! We've got to tell Page!"

Monica charged into the living room. Page

was watching a rock concert on TV. "Page! *Page!*" she hollered.

Page's legs were propped against the TV stand, balancing a bowl of popcorn. She jumped up and popcorn flew everywhere. "Monica!" Page wailed. "Look what you made me do!"

"Never mind, Page," Monica cried. "You've got to come with me to the garden. Now! The Bramley Wildcat is in the tool-shed!"

"What?" Page yelled. "Monica, are you kidding around with me?"

Monica grabbed Page's arm and began to drag her toward the back door. "No, Page," Monica begged. "Honest."

Dee Ellen was standing by the little bathroom off the kitchen "What is it?" she asked as they stumbled by. "Who's out there?"

"Our piggy-bank robber!" Monica shouted. "That's who. And it isn't a weredog or a wildcat or a spooky cocker spaniel. It's somebody dressed up!"

"Oh," Dee Ellen said. She began to slide through the bathroom door.

"Dee Ellen!" Monica screamed. "Aren't you coming with us? It's time for the naked truth!"

"I've got to go to the bathroom," Dee Ellen said.

Monica couldn't believe it. Right when things got exciting, her partner headed for the bathroom.

Page was at the back door. "Come on, Monica," she called. "I want to see what's in that toolshed."

Monica couldn't wait another second. She flew through the door and clattered down the steps to the patio. Page was already crossing the moonlit garden.

The statues made dark, twisting shapes on the grassy lawn. Monica made her feet pound over them. From far away she heard drums beating and music playing. The parade would be starting soon.

The toolshed was just ahead and Page was

already at the door. "The lock's undone," Page said when Monica trotted up. "Somebody's been in here."

Together they crept into the shadowy shed. Patches of moonlight fell through a dirt-streaked window. Monica's eyes zoomed over the pots, cans, and garden tools. "There on the floor," she whispered. "Isn't that a jacket?"

Page lifted a Bramley High School jacket from the floor. "There's a name on the tag," she said. "But it's all curled up."

Page fiddled with the label as Monica stood glued to her side. "It says Brian Abbott," Page finally read.

"Brian *Abbott?*" Monica croaked. "You mean the kid who works for the Zellers? Is that Nola's brother?"

Page nodded and looked at her. The dim light made her eyes a deep dark blue. "Mm-hmmm," she said. "And he's the vice-president of the senior class."

A small whining creak sounded behind

them. Shivers chugged through Monica's body. Together, she and Page slowly turned their heads.

Standing in the doorway was a large yellow beast.

"Grrrrrrr." A deep rumbling growl rolled from its open mouth.

CHAPTER NINE

Something shiny flashed in the wide growling mouth.

"Brian Abbott!" Monica cried. "That's you, isn't it? You've been hiding the Bramley Wildcat in this toolshed!"

Puffy paws reached up and pulled off the wildcat head. Underneath was the sweaty face of the boy who worked for the Zellers. "Exactly right," he said. "I guess my growl didn't scare you."

"I'm not scared of a beast wearing braces," Monica snapped.

Brian's eyes got thin and squinty. "Well,

hi, Page," he said. "I figured your snoopy sister would end up bringing you around."

Monica stomped one step closer. "And what about *your* sister?" she asked. "You tried to take Nola's birthday money."

"Awwwww," Brian said. "I got sick of her bragging about it. I just wanted to scare her a little."

"I want that costume," Page suddenly said. "And so does Kirby."

Brian lifted his arms until he completely filled the open doorway. "Sorry," he said. He lifted the wildcat head back over his own. "It's time for this wildcat to go on the prowl."

For a split second the doorway was an empty shape. Then the shape went black and a sound boomed in Monica's ears. It was followed by a string of soft, dull clicks.

"Monica!" Page shrieked. "He's locked us in!"

Monica whirled right and left, blinking in the darkness. "The window!" she hollered, diving across the room. She looked up—way up at the dirt-streaked glass.

Page bent and made a cup with her hands. "Quick—I'll give you a lift," she said.

Page boosted Monica onto her shoulders. Monica curled her fingers over the top edge of the window and pulled. "It's stuck!" Monica wailed "It won't move!"

"Try harder," Page begged.

Through the dusty glass Monica saw Brian trying to waddle through the garden. He was having a little trouble with the wildcat's big, puffy feet.

Then she saw Dee Ellen. She was standing on the back steps that led to the patio.

"Dee Ellen!" Monica screamed. "Stop him! That's Brian in the Bramley Wildcat costume!"

A yellow car pulled into the Zellers' circular driveway. "Hey, Brian," called the driver. "Hurry! We've got to get you to the parade."

"No!" Monica shrieked. "They'll help him get away! Do something, Dee Ellen!"

Dee Ellen looked as if she were frozen to

the steps. *Has her mind turned to mush?* Monica wondered. Could she even move?

Monica gripped the window edge again and tried to rock it up and down.

"Hey!" Page shouted from below. "Watch it!"

Suddenly Monica was rocking one way and Page the other. She was stretching out— out—over open air.

The window shuddered, and with a lurch, fell farther open. Monica fell, too. The next thing she knew, she and Page were in a jumble on the floor.

"Oooo," Page groaned. "You knocked the wind out of me."

Monica scrambled off her sister and began to hop up and down. "It's open enough now," Monica said. "Boost me again, Page! We can't let Brian get away!"

Page lifted Monica again. This time she was able to shimmy out the window and drop to the ground.

When Monica looked toward the house, she couldn't believe what she saw.

Dee Ellen wasn't frozen on the steps. She was nowhere in sight. And Brian wasn't making his getaway. He'd only made it up to the patio. He wasn't trying to run anymore. Monica wasn't sure what Brian was doing.

As she watched, one huge foot jerked up into the air. Then another. Brian looked as if he were doing a strange, hopping kind of dance.

What is going on? Monica wondered. Had the beast stopped to rock, bop, and boogey on the Zellers' patio?

CHAPTER TEN

Page was wriggling through the toolshed window. She swung one leg out, then both. Then she dropped onto the grass beside Monica. "Run!" Page cried, and they both took off for the patio.

As they ran, headlights flashed in their faces. Mr. Zeller's car turned into the driveway and the yellow car zoomed away.

Finally, Monica and Page reached the patio. The wildcat had just flipped into the air and fallen onto the stone tiles. He waved a puffy paw at them. "She threw big marbles at me!" Brian hollered. "She made me trip on all those marbles!"

Dee Ellen stepped from behind a bush. "It wasn't marbles," she said. "I saw him coming, so I threw the necklace. The shoelaces broke."

Monica looked down. There, scattered across the Zellers' patio, were all the lumpy little balls of garlic.

"The garlic!" Monica cried. "That was quick thinking, Dee Ellen! That took brain power!"

Mr. Zeller pushed through the lilac bushes. "What are you all doing out here?" he demanded. "Whatever is going on?"

Monica stepped forward. "Brian Abbott's been hiding the school mascot in your toolshed. Whoever finds it gets to ride on the school float!"

Mr. Zeller looked from face to face and back again. Then he chuckled and pulled Brian to his feet. "I see," he said. "Well, Brian. It looks as if you've been found."

"Don't fire me, Mr. Zeller," Brian begged.

"I didn't mean to scare anybody. Just my stupid sister."

"Off with the costume now," Mr. Zeller ordered.

Brian took off the puffy yellow paws. Then he began pulling at buttons on the front of the costume. One piece came off like a shirt. The other was pants with a tail sewn onto the back.

Monica stared at the rumpled costume lying in the grass. "How about that?" she said. "That isn't even real fur. Somebody painted stripes onto a pair of pajamas."

"And I thought that was Rocky's ghost," Dee Ellen said. She looked at Monica. "You must have thought I was pretty silly."

Suddenly Monica knew exactly what she'd thought. "I thought your house was taking over your brain. Just like that story in *The National Star.*"

Mr. Zeller put a hand on Dee Ellen's shoulder. "Didn't I warn you about stories, Dee Ellen? Didn't I say they'd just cause trouble?"

Monica hung her head. The stories had caused a lot of trouble. And she'd been as bad as everyone else. She'd even started the story about Rocky.

"I guess we weren't very logical," Monica said in a tiny voice.

"I guess not," said Mr. Zeller.

Page scooped all the costume pieces up into her arms. Then she and Brian talked to Mr. Zeller some more.

"Mr. Zeller's going to drive us to the schoolyard," Page called to her sister. "I hope we're not too late. Come on, Monica, hurry. This is really important!"

Monica and Dee Ellen followed the others to the Zellers' car. Monica had never seen Page so excited. She didn't even care that her hair wasn't combed.

But Monica felt pretty darn droopy. This case wasn't going to make the Ketchup Sisters famous. *The National Star* wouldn't want a story about somebody's old pajamas.

CHAPTER ELEVEN

A crowd of kids ran to meet the car at the school grounds. Monica peered into the night as Page climbed out. Behind the crowd, Monica saw the pep rally float. It was decorated with twisted streamers and red and white balloons.

A few moments later Page was back. "Come ride with us, Monica," she hollered. "Kirby says you two get the best seats on the float!"

Monica opened the door and stumbled out. "But why?" she said.

"Because you stopped Brian from getting

here first!" Page said. "Here they are," she called to the crowd. "The Ketchup Sisters! Thanks to them, the juniors get to ride the float this year!"

"Ketch-Up! Ketch-Up!" the juniors all yelled. They were raising fists high into the air.

Monica looked from the cheering crowd to her smiling sister. Page's eyes were gleaming with pride. "Oh, Page," Monica whispered. "Listen to that. The Ketchup Sisters are famous after all."

"Well, maybe a little," Page said, laughing. "And just for tonight. Tomorrow all they'll care about is the football game."

Kirby leaned over the back edge of the float. He was wearing the top and bottom to the wildcat costume. "Come on, Monica," he shouted. "I'll give you a boost."

Monica turned back to the car. "Dee Ellen!" she cried. "Didn't you hear that? Why are you still sitting there?"

Dee Ellen inched forward on the seat. She

had the perfectly miserable look on her face again.

Oh no, Monica worried. Her partner hated crowds. How would she ever get Dee Ellen to like being famous?

"Will there be food there?" Dee Ellen asked.

"Tons of it," Page said. "At the bonfire party."

Dee Ellen climbed out of the car. The front of her sweatshirt said CLEAN AND SUDSY LAUNDRY CENTERS. "Okay, I'm coming," she mumbled.

Monica let out a big whooshing breath of air. Maybe it wouldn't be so hard. She'd just pack plenty of snacks from now on. Then the Ketchup Sisters could work on getting really famous.

And they wouldn't have to worry about stomach cramps.

About the Author and Illustrator

JUDITH HOLLANDS graduated from Boston University and has taught elementary school and gifted education. She says that she decided to write *The Ketchup Sisters* after she learned that "my daughter and her friend wanted to become blood sisters but neither of them wanted to deal with the blood. They came up with the idea of using ketchup and christened themselves 'The Ketchup Sisters.' I decided to jot down that title because it made me laugh. I told them then: 'I'll have to use that in a story.' " Ms. Hollands has also written *Bowser the Beautiful, The Nerve of Abbey Mars,* and *The Like Potion,* all available in Minstrel Books. She is married with two children, and owns two dogs, two cats, and three horses. The family recently moved to a thirty-three-acre horse farm.

DEE DEROSA grew up in Colorado, graduated from Syracuse University, and now lives in a rural area of New York State. She is married and has two children, three horses, and one dog. Ms. deRosa also illustrated *Bowser the Beautiful* and *The Nerve of Abbey Mars.*

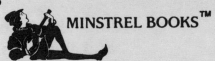

____THE DASTARDLY MURDER OF DIRTY PETE
     Eth Clifford 68859/$2.75
____ME, MY GOAT, AND MY SISTER'S WEDDING
     Stella Pevsner 66206/$2.75
____DANGER ON PANTHER PEAK
     Bill Marshall 70271/$2.95
____BOWSER THE BEAUTIFUL
     Judith Hollands 70488/$2.75
____THE MONSTER'S RING
     Bruce Colville 69389/$2.75
____KEVIN CORBETT EATS FLIES
     Patricia Hermes 69183/$2.95
____ROSY COLE'S GREAT AMERICAN GUILT CLUB
     Sheila Greenwald 70864/$2.75
____ROSY'S ROMANCE Sheila Greenwald 70292/$2.75
____WRITE ON, ROSY! Sheila Greenwald 68569/$2.75
____ME AND THE TERRIBLE TWO Ellen Conford 68491/$2.75
____SNOT STEW Bill Wallace 69335/$2.75
____WHO NEEDS A BRATTY BROTHER?
     Linda Gondosh 62777/$2.50
____FERRET IN THE BEDROOM, LIZARDS IN THE FRIDGE
     Bill Wallace 68009/$2.75
____THE CASE OF THE VISITING VAMPIRE
     Drew Stevenson 65732/$2.50
____THE WITCHES OF HOPPER STREET
     Linda Gondosch 64066/$2.50
____HARVEY THE BEER CAN KING Jamie Gilson 67423/$2.50
____ALVIN WEBSTER'S SUREFIRE PLAN FOR SUCCESS
     (AND HOW IT FAILED) Sheila Greenwald 67239/$2.75
____THE KETCHUP SISTERS:
     THE RESCUE OF THE RED-BLOODED LIBRARIAN
     Judith Hollands 66810/$2.75
____THE KETCHUP SISTERS:
     THE SECRET OF THE HAUNTED DOGHOUSE
     Judith Hollands 66812/$2.75

Simon & Schuster Mail Order Department MMM
200 Old Tappan Rd., Old Tappan, N.J. 07675
Please send me the books I have checked above. I am enclosing $_____ (please add 75¢ to
cover postage and handling for each order. N.Y.S. and N.Y.C. residents please add appropriate
sales tax). Send check or money order—no cash or C.O.D.'s please. Allow up to six weeks for
delivery. For purchases over $10.00 you may use VISA: card number, expiration date and
customer signature must be included.

Name _____

Address _____

City _____ State/Zip _____

VISA Card No. _____ Exp. Date _____

Signature _____ 184-17

MEET THE *NEW* BOBBSEY TWINS™

THE BOBBSEY TWINS ARE BACK
AND BETTER THAN EVER!

When older twins Nan and Bert and younger twins Freddie and Flossie get into mischief, there's no end to the mystery and adventure.

Join the Bobbsey twins as they track down clues, escape danger, and unravel mysteries in these brand-new, fun-filled stories.

The *New* Bobbsey Twins:

__	#1 The Secret of Jungle Park	62651	$2.95
__	#2 The Case of the Runaway Money	62652	$2.95
__	#3 The Clue That Flew Away	62653	$2.95
__	#4 The Secret in the Sand Castle	62654	$2.95
__	#5 The Case of the Close Encounter	62656	$2.95
__	#6 Mystery on the Mississippi	62657	$2.95
__	#7 Trouble in Toyland	62658	$2.95
__	#8 The Secret of the Stolen Puppies	62659	$2.95
__	#9 The Clue In The Classroom	63072	$2.95
__	#10 The Chocolate-Covered Clue	63073	$2.95
__	#11 The Case of the Crooked Contest	63074	$2.95
__	#12 The Secret Of The Sunken Treasure	63075	$2.95
__	#13 The Case Of The Crying Clown	55501	$2.95
__	#14 The Mystery Of The Missing Mummy	67595	$3.50
__	#15 The Secret of the Stolen Clue	67596	$2.95
__	#16 The Case of the Missing Dinosaur 67597 $2.95		
__	#17 The Case at Creepy Castle 69289 $2.95		

MINSTREL BOOKS™